HOLLOW BONES

B. NARR

HOLLOW BONES

Copyright © 2019 by B. Narr

For information go to:
http://www.bnarr.com

Cover design by Eric C. Wilder
Photography by Jasmine Aurora Poole
Edited by Ryan Boyd
ISBN: 978-1-7340218-0-6
e-ISBN: 978-1-7340218-1-3

First Edition: October 2019

Printed in the United States of America.

TABLE OF CONTENTS

DEDICATION 1

PROLOGUE 2

GREENBRIER 7

BIG BAYOU 15

BIRD BONES 26

VITAL SIGNS 34

NIGHT SONG 42

RANGER STATION 52

WORK ZONE 64

OUT THERE 69

ON RECORD 76

SHOTGUN SHELLS 88

DRY ROT 96

DARK WATERS 102

AFTERMATH 114

ABOUT THE AUTHOR 119

ACKNOWLEDGEMENTS 120

Thank you to all the amazing biologists who inspired this book.

I hope you never get eaten by monsters.

PROLOGUE

The predawn darkness simmered. Frogs trilled from the tops of cypress trees, harmonizing with cicadas and mosquitos. The Evans boys tried to make their steps blend in with the swamp hum, avoiding prematurely dry leaves and twigs with their clunky muck boots. To Mason, every step felt sluggish. The drought had brought with it heat even more suffocating than usual – he was cooking in his hunting gear. Why Sawyer had insisted that they fully suit up for a squirrel hunt, he would never understand. It's not like camo ever worked on squirrels. They didn't need to see you to know when to run.

Sawyer knew that, too. They'd been hunting together for years, mostly bushytails. Squirrels weren't necessarily the most impressive-looking quarry, but in reality, they were a challenge. Someday, Mason thought, they'd upgrade to something even harder. Maybe wild boars. Those were always in season. Then the full gear would be necessary. Right now, it felt like playing dress-up. He suspected his older brother was doing it for a picture. Sawyer was starting high school in the fall and had been talking about impressing girls with his hunting skills. Mason wasn't so sure that would work. All the girls in Uncertain knew him already. One summer wouldn't change that, and neither would a picture of him in ill-fitting camo swiped from their dad's closet. He should just give them some squirrel jerky and hope for the best.

Voicing that never worked out well, though, so Mason kept his mouth shut. At least they were hunting together. Sorta. They hadn't really gotten to the hunting part yet. They'd been walking for what seemed like ages now, and they still hadn't gotten to the creek they'd heard about. It was supposed to be the best place to squirrel hunt around here – hell, it was the only place at this point. Everywhere else within fifty miles of Caddo Lake had been sold off to some land development company or oil company or something. Mason couldn't remember exactly. He just remembered the pang of loss he felt when he heard the only place they'd ever hunted was getting cleared. Shaved down clean to the dirt and made into something unrecognizable.

"You sure we're still going the right way?" Mason finally asked.

"'Course I am," Sawyer said, his voice barely above a whisper. "Now shhh."

Mason dropped into a whisper, too, but not as quiet as his brother. "'Cause I still haven't heard no running water–"

"Mase, I said shhhh. You're gonna scare off every squirrel here."

"How am I gonna scare off the squirrels? We ain't even seen one yet."

"That's 'cause you walk too loud."

"Do not. You walk too loud."

"I do not–"

There was a rustle up ahead. The boys quieted and aimed their rifles at the noise reflexively. The argument could wait. It was one of those perpetual sibling arguments that could go on for hours without a mediator and that had been popping up periodically since both of them could talk. The argument could always wait. Squirrels were rarely so patient. You got one shot with most critters, especially the small ones. They'd be gone in the time it took to reload.

Underbrush rustled up ahead again, and Mason realized there was no other noise around them. The bayou had fallen utterly silent with them. As he steadied his sights on the tree line, he saw something approaching. Something big. Mason's stomach dropped. Despite the suffocating heat, a chill ran through him.

He caught his brother's gaze. They weren't prepared for anything big. They only had .22s, for god's sake, and those could hardly kill a coyote unless you knew exactly where to aim.

"It's gonna be alright. Just. Stay calm." Sawyer had his big brother voice now. That calm bravado. But as Sawyer aimed his rifle higher, Mason saw the blood had drained from his face.

Mason nodded and readjusted his own gun. The noise grew closer, and with it came a gust of hot, rancid wind. Mason tasted death in the back of his throat. His stomach clenched. His grip shook on the stock, his palms slick with sweat. He wanted to look over at his brother for reassurance again, but he couldn't tear his eyes away from the unnatural gait of the thing approaching them. For a merciful second, Mason thought it might just be an injured buck, but he quickly realized it was the wrong color, wrong proportions. Bone-white and emaciated, flesh hanging off it in ribbons, it strode towards them like a ghost. Mason knew they'd missed their chance to run – that maybe they'd never had one – and dug his heels into the hard ground, trying to mimic his brother's stance, trying to think of something to say; he didn't want arguing to be the last thing they ever did.

GREENBRIER

The mallet hung heavy in Luca Navarro's hand. She thought swamps were supposed to be all soft, pliable mud. The ground here was hard as rock. She was starting to think it might actually be rock. It had taken almost five minutes to hammer in the piece of rebar she needed to set up mist nets, and she had four more pieces to go for this set alone.

Normally, mist nets were easy to put up. When the ground gave way and there wasn't much brush-clearing to do, Luca and her fellow ornithologist, Danielle Wright, could assemble a dozen before the sun rose over the trees. That was the best time to get it done – just as the world was waking up, before the sun shone in full and the nets really did seem to disappear like mist. Too much later, she and Danielle's presence – loud and human – would ruin their chances of catching any birds in the area. It's not as if they could wait there and politely ask them for blood samples. Birds weren't keen on doing anything that involved getting trapped, even if they were going to get let go later. Luca hardly blamed them.

As Luca got the second rebar into the ground, Danielle trotted up the trail. Bags of nets hung from her arms and hollow metal poles clinked together as she carried them over her shoulder. They rattled louder as she shook a black ringlet out of her eyes.

"I seriously need to braid my hair once we're done with this, it's already killing me." Danielle wore her hair in a soft cloud of curls when she wasn't in the field, and sometimes when she was – only on particularly humid days did she need to braid it back. There were a lot of humid days in Caddo Lake. Luca just cropped her hair to her skull every field season and called it good.

"Once we get these last few sets of nets up, I say we head back to camp. Then you can do that, and I can make coffee."

"Yesss!" Danielle did a little fist pump, but only got halfway through it before the poles began to slip. She quickly righted them. "I love that Greca you've got more than life itself."

"I know, right? I'd probably die for it at this point."

"No one could blame you for dying for coffee."

Technically, the metal brewer made espresso, not coffee, but no one could tell from the way they drank it. Camping mugs were filled to the brim every morning, sometimes twice. Luca usually regretted the second cup. That never stopped her, of course. The long hours weren't easy to pull off, waking up before dawn and going to bed after dark, and they had been doing it for three weeks straight now. It wasn't a schedule they'd planned for. They were exhausted, their funds were stretched thin, and soon they would have lab work to get back to. By all accounts, they should have been done – but they'd been asked a favor too important to ignore.

The folks who took care of the Caddo Lake Wildlife Management Area needed help. Local government had sold off almost 1,000 acres of it to an oil company for pipeline construction and deemed the

WMA not useful – they were planning to sell more if someone couldn't prove otherwise. Conserving habitats for local wildlife wasn't useful enough, apparently, and neither was the slow trickle of tourism the WMA afforded. Visiting researchers were their last hope to regain legitimacy. The WMA managers had scoured biology lab websites for contacts, and Luca and Danielle were the only ones who had agreed to come on such short notice. Governments weren't always keen on listening to scientists, of course, but it was better than nothing.

It might have been different if they didn't already have a Texas permit, or if they'd been further away than southeastern Oklahoma, or if they hadn't been able to easily extend their disease study to encompass northeast Texas. They might have said no. Hell, they might have missed the call entirely if they'd been in a place with less signal. But as it stood, they had headed straight to Caddo Lake, just outside of Uncertain, Texas. The three-hour drive was all bitter gas station coffee and Fleetwood Mac blasting out of open windows, the latter being Danielle's idea. It had done more to keep the fatigue at bay than Luca had expected. Even now, as they put up nets, she found herself humming.

Today was their first day in the WMA, which barely counted as a day of research. It was mostly a day of set-up and exploration. Setting up camp, clearing paths, stringing nets. Finding good places for nets always took the longest – especially in a swamp. Nothing was as it seemed out here. Ground that should be solid swallowed their feet whole, and ground that looked soft was a facade for rocks lying just below the surface. Eastern Ratsnakes hung Christmas-light-style above them in trees, indistinguishable from thick vines and branches. Scrubby, hidden weeds snatched at their clothes like hands. *No further*, they whispered, *go back*.

But Luca never went back. Instead, with each set of nets, she and Danielle pressed deeper into the swamp, using machetes to clear the way before they hauled more poles out.

"There, that looks promising." Danielle pointed her machete at what looked like an old deer trail, blocked only by greenbrier. "Prickly, but promising."

Where greenbrier was, there was often little else in the way of undergrowth to deal with. It choked the life out of other plants, dominating the landscape with its soft, thorny vines; it was easy to cut and edible to boot. Greenbrier was a best-case scenario as far as Luca was concerned. While they started hacking a path through it, Luca picked off a leaf and popped it into her mouth.

Instead of the bright spinach crunch she expected, it was flimsy and bitter. Wrong. She spit it out.

Danielle turned back to look at her. "What's wrong?"

"It tastes like it's gone bad." Luca wished that she had some of the coffee they'd talked about, just to get the acrid twang out of her mouth.

"Weird. I didn't think things could go bad while they were still alive."

"I guess they can." Luca nudged a nearby vine, and it cracked like a dry twig. "Or maybe it's not alive."

Danielle followed suit with a vine in front of her. It crumbled. "Ohhh, yikes. It's not supposed to do that this time of year. Or any time, I think."

The greenbrier got worse with every step down the trail until it wasn't green at all, but a sickly brown. Dead. And with it, the noise in the swamp died. Eventually, the only thing Luca could hear was the crunch of dried vines under their feet and her own breathing. She had never been somewhere so utterly still. Then she heard Danielle clap a hand over her mouth, and she felt it. A hot wind blowing up from just beyond the end of the trail, rustling the dry underbrush and bringing with it the smell of rot. Luca nearly gagged.

"What the hell…" Luca pulled her shirt collar up over her face.

"… Do you wanna look first?" The question had nothing to do with how much or how little Luca wanted to do anything. Danielle's free hand was fiddling nervously with her machete, and she was inching back towards Luca.

"Sure." Slowly, Luca stepped in front and brushed aside the last of the dead greenbrier to reveal a clearing – and the source of the smell.

Strewn across the clearing were the corpses of dozens of songbirds. They were all different species, a morbid rainbow of ragged feathers, and they looked like they'd been out there for days. Luca and Danielle stopped cold. It raised the hairs on the back of Luca's neck like nails down a chalkboard. Bird carcasses rarely lasted more than a few hours in the wilderness.

Scavengers would snatch up the free meal eagerly, or pick their little bodies clean where they lay. Yet here they were, untouched *en masse*. A monument to decay. Luca crouched to inspect them, to see what had killed them, but it looked for all the world like they had just dried up.

BIG BAYOU

The tributaries were gone. Half of the bayou was gone. In the middle of what had to be the most sudden drought on record, Harper Benoit and her dad, Gerald, had found themselves hauling the last tourists' boat out of knee-deep mud where water should have been. "Big Bayou Swamp Tours!" wasn't going to be back in business any time soon.

Up until then, the Benoits had been the best swamp tour guides in Uncertain. Maybe even the whole Caddo Lake area, a wetland that sprawled all the way from Texas to Louisiana. But it was hard to be a swamp tour guide without a swamp.

Some people in town had insisted they take the drought as an opportunity to shut down tours for a little while — to avoid leading outsiders through the swamp until someone found those missing boys. It was a more serious police investigation than the residents of Uncertain were used to, so no one was sure what measures they should be taking. People disappeared around Caddo Lake from time to time, sure, but they were never locals. Especially not armed locals. It had people jumpy.

And then there were the construction crews. Not only did that mean extra outsiders, extra reasons to be nervous, but disruptions, too. Crews had been peppered around the swamp for an oil company's pipeline project that ran clear through the whole place, creating jarring industrial breaks from the nature people were paying to experience. Harper was sure it would lose them return customers.

The fact of the matter, though, was that the Benoits couldn't afford to stop, regardless of the construction, or where Mason and Sawyer Evans had gone off to. They had payments to make. Food to buy. As long as the police weren't closing off that part of Big Cypress Bayou, the Benoits weren't shutting down. They would simply have to rebrand.

After some deliberation, they replaced the old boat tours with "Big Bayou Hiking Tours! Fishing included!" Most people didn't take them up on the fishing. Between out-of-towners having to pay extra for fishing licenses and the prospect of lugging the gear almost five miles, Harper couldn't blame them. She wasn't a fan of this whole hiking business in general. It was a hell of a lot more laborious than swamp tours, and the people were harder to keep track of when they weren't all crammed into a boat.

Today's group was smaller than usual, especially for one this close to Memorial Day weekend. Only four, all young. College students, Harper figured, judging from their age and the assorted Greek life T-shirts. They had predictably opted out of the fishing.

To keep better track of the tourists, her dad led the group and Harper brought up the back – someone to lead and someone to usher stragglers along. It was a good system. The last few times they had done this, people had hardly talked to Harper, and she liked it that way. Her dad was the tour guide here. Spouting fun facts was second nature to him, always had been. She could recite his favorites by heart, but never did. He was better at talking to people. A lot of tourists picked up on his friendly nature and took to chatting with him, and these were no exception. Half of them had spent the whole hike quizzing Gerald. One was a lithe girl with buck teeth and dewy eyes that reminded Harper of a deer. The other, a chipper blonde, was the only person wearing hiking boots rather than sandals.

"Are we gonna hear any whippoorwills?" The blonde asked, "I know it's still like, daytime, but I've seen videos where they do that."

"You just wanna hear one because of that Randy Travis song," the deer girl rolled her eyes.

"Oh, shut up," the blonde swatted at the deer girl's arm.

"Nope," Gerald shook his head, "Hate to break it to you, but we're too far west for that." A wild thing to say when you could spit and hit Louisiana, but it was true. "You might hear a Chuck Will's Widow, though." Gerald continued. "They're the whippoorwill's less-famous cousin."

"Chuck Will's Widow? Sounds sad." The deer girl said. "Why would they name a bird that?"

"For the song it sings." Gerald whistled, low and mournful. A perfect imitation of the night bird itself. "It's the only bird you're gonna hear out here at night other than a stray owl." Then he quickly added, "And maybe during the day, too, if we're lucky."

The last part wasn't true. Not in the slightest. But Harper's dad wasn't in the business of disappointing people. He would always rather tell a nice lie than an uncomfortable truth, however mild the discomfort would be.

As soon as his answer went over well with the group, Harper turned her attention back to the trail. From somewhere in the trees a familiar bitter musk wafted: a cottonmouth. She saw it a moment later, slithering across the trail just behind her feet, mottled back nearly invisible against the swamp floor. Harper held her breath. Hot weather made the already-territorial snakes snappy, and they were miles from the nearest hospital. A tourist with a snakebite was the last thing they needed.

She watched to make sure the snake actually left, and she almost missed two of the tourists veering to the right. Normally, that wouldn't be an issue. The trail was relatively wide, they could bob and weave as much as they wanted as long as they stayed on it. But that was the problem. They weren't.

"Dude, check that out. That's weird." One of them, a bulky guy with perfectly smooth legs, said. He was pointing to an offshoot trail. One that hadn't been there last hike, Harper noted. It looked like someone had sprayed weed killer to form it. All the plants that should be covering it were withered and dead.

The other hiker, a guy sporting a fancy camera and a neon tank that said *Suns Out, Guns Out*, oohed softly at it.

"I bet I could get some sweet pictures for that photography class in there," he said. He'd been snapping pictures the whole hike.

"God, you're such a tryhard." The smooth-legged guy slapped him on the back, "Classes don't even start 'til August."

"You're just jealous 'cause I'll be done early and you won't." The photographer smirked and returned the gesture as he wandered in.

"Hey, now, stay on the trail." Harper finally called out.

"I'll just be a second." The photographer completely ignored her, stepping over the skeletal husks of greenbrier.

"Son, she's serious. It ain't safe in there. Come on back." Gerald attempted to wave him back, but to no avail. The photographer had already disappeared into the trees.

"I'm sorry, I'll go with him to make sure he doesn't do anything stupid," the smooth-legged guy reassured them, which was not reassuring at all. "I shouldn't have mentioned it to his dumb ass in the first place."

"Ugh, why does he always do this?" The deer girl ran a hand down her face, then shouted after them, "You better not get us kicked off another tour, Ryan!" Harper didn't know which one was Ryan, but she figured it was the photographer.

"Now no one's gonna get kicked off nothing, but no one needs to follow him." Gerald was using his dad voice now. Not that it had any effect on the two who had already left. "I'm gonna go get 'em, you two stay right here with Harper."

The remaining tourists nodded as Gerald disappeared into the trees. Harper stepped up to be beside them, rather than behind. Anxious tension buzzed around the girls like gnats.

"... So, your friend does this often?" Harper asked. Conversation was a good distraction, even if she wasn't a huge fan of it.

"All the time." The deer girl rolled her eyes.

"Last time, he got us kicked off a Grand Canyon hike for trying to –" A *crack* came from just beyond the trees and the blonde stopped with a gasp. "What was that?" She looked at Harper, wide-eyed, for answers.

Harper opened her mouth to speak when a sickening *thunk* echoed through the swamp. Then a scream, one of the boys', followed by a gunshot. Her dad always carried a gun when they gave tours — dangerous things lived out here, but never once had she known him to use it. Her heart leapt into her throat.

"Ryan!" The deer girl bolted towards the noise. Harper grabbed her arm to stop her, but the girl yanked out of her grip with a glare. "Don't fucking touch me, I'm gonna go help them!"

"No, it's not safe –" Harper started, but deer girl was already gone. Fantastic. She looked over at the blonde who was still frozen with indecision. To her own surprise, she kept her voice even. "Alright, I guess we're all going in there, c'mon."

Without waiting for a response, Harper ushered the blonde with her onto the path. Another gunshot rang out like distant thunder. A scream, she wasn't sure whose. A second later Harper was running, the blonde not far behind. The swamp was a blur of dying leaves and bony cypress as she followed the sound of commotion. Something else simmered under the yelling, under the deafening rustle of ground cover. A radiator hiss layered over itself a hundred times. Harper couldn't place it.

She and the blonde skidded to a stop in a clearing that was bigger than she'd expected. And drier. Dust was, impossibly, billowing up in clouds under their feet. It was thick, so thick Harper couldn't breathe. The air around them reeked of death. The blonde coughed and cursed behind her. Through the haze, she could make out human figures. All but one was on the ground, rag dolls sprawled across the dry dirt. The only one still standing was lithe, deer girl, trying to drag up one of the bodies. Behind her, another figure moved. A much taller one, teetering on four bony legs.

The *thing*, unnaturally proportioned and covered in something that hung off it like torn flesh, stepped forward with jerky, forced movements. It bucked its bone-white head at the deer girl before she could dodge and flung her across the clearing. She landed with a sickening crack. That was enough to jerk Harper out of stunned silence to turn to the blonde.

"Go, go, get out!" Harper urged her away from the chaotic scene, but the blonde was already running to where deer girl had landed. It was hard to blame her. Harper was about to call out for her father when the creature opened its toothy maw and made a noise like a wildfire roaring in the wind.

Harper felt herself running again before she told her legs to start. Heavy work boots kicked up more dust in her wake. She scanned the figures as she passed them until she found the one she recognized most: a gangly man in overalls. He'd been tossed to the edge of the clearing, probably the same way as deer girl. Harper's chest tightened.

"Dad!"

He didn't respond. It wasn't until Harper was right up on him that she heard him mumbling, trying in vain to get up. He was saying something about being fine — a nice lie. Before she could start to comfort him, or tell him to save his breath, a gurgling scream in the distance cut her off. The blonde. It had to be her. There was no one else left.

The thought set her stomach churning. She didn't have long to dwell on it. Those uneven hoofbeats were getting closer now. Harper hoisted her dad into a fireman's carry and scrambled out of the clearing. She didn't stop. Not when she heard groaning from one of the tourists, not when the leaves finally stopped rustling behind her. Through underbrush, through muck, through tangled trees, she kept going until her shoulders burned and her lungs ached. No matter how far she got, the creature's raspy howl drilled into her skull; but it couldn't drown out the screams of the people she had left behind, or the encroaching guilt that threatened to bury her alive.

BIRD BONES

"Do you have signal yet?" Out of the corner of her eye, Danielle saw Luca waving her phone back-and-forth, then stick her hand out the window to get it higher.

"Nope. Still nothing. So just… Keep driving, I guess."

It took a solid ten minutes to get out of the WMA in the field truck. Finding somewhere with signal took even longer. It was an agonizing search. Every minute they wasted was a minute that a scavenger could carry off one of the bird's carcasses — if they waited too long, they'd have no evidence to show the WMA managers that something was very, very wrong.

Danielle was starting to think that Marion County was completely devoid of cell towers. Aside from a few isolated farms, the closest piece of civilization was Uncertain, a town that had a population of 94 and dropping. The only place either of them got reliable signal was the ranger station in the state park. Outside of that, it was radio silence until the next city. Normally that didn't bother her. Danielle, like every other scientist who had done fieldwork, was used to isolation. But that usually didn't extend beyond the field site. Here, even the roads were quiet.

"Got it!" Luca had her neck craned, phone pressed up against the ceiling of the cab. "Find somewhere to pull over, quick, it's one bar."

"Ooone sec, one sec." Danielle slowed the truck to a crawl, whiteknuckling the wheel as she looked for a turnoff. Making snap decisions always ramped up her anxiety, even if it wasn't an emergency, and this felt close enough to an emergency that it was even worse. As soon as she could, she whipped into a long-abandoned pasture entrance and tried to exhale.

The field truck was a hulking beast of burden with what may have been the widest turn radius in vehicular history. It took Danielle longer to get its ass out of the road than it took for Luca to have an entire conversation with the WMA managers. By the time she'd gotten in a good spot, she had to pull right back out again.

The WMA managers beat them to the gates, but they waited to be led to the campsite. After that, it was all on foot. There weren't many places to drive in the 8,000-acre wilderness. Between swamp water and hidden ditches and impermeable cypress, most paths only let you in – they didn't let you out. More than once, Danielle had had the unsettling thought of driving the wrong way and sinking to the bottom of the swamp. She had seen the end results of that in the tucked away corners of the bayou. Titans from decades past, buildings and vehicles and things less recognizable, eaten alive by the earth.

"Y'know, this is the first we've heard of this kinda thing," said one of WMA managers, Sydney. She was a wiry woman with the thickest Southern accent Danielle had ever heard, and she had come armed with baggies. They were for temporary specimen storage, she'd said.

Which was fair. Danielle and Luca couldn't do much with rotting carcasses. She wasn't sure that Sydney was going to want them once she saw them, though.

"And you said there weren't any visible injuries?" said the other, Doug, a middle-aged man with an already-graying push-broom mustache. It fluttered with every word, as if it was the one speaking. "Because that's the part that gets me. Other than, well, the fact that they're out here at all."

"Yeah, me too," said Sydney, "'Cause there's no way a hunter could kill a buncha songbirds that clean."

"I doubt the hunters around here would be stupid enough to illegally kill songbirds, anyway," Doug added, "I doubt anyone would. Had to be an animal, or maybe blunt force trauma."

"I just don't get why it wouldn't eat 'em," Sydney said, "Unless it only ate parts, like possums. Did they still have heads?"

"It looked like most of them did, if not all of them," said Luca, nudging a fallen branch out of their way. She and Danielle hadn't exactly finished clearing the path yet. "It almost looked like something had just knocked them out of the trees and they'd died there. Which doesn't make a lot of sense, frankly."

"No, but I wouldn't rule out anything yet," said Doug, "Especially not with what you said about the plants and all."

"Yeah, we were gonna ask you about that," said Danielle, "Is there anything around here that could be contaminating the groundwater or the soil? Like runoff or anything like that?"

"Not that I know of," said Doug, "No industrial farms or factories anywhere near here. The pipeline construction is a few miles off, but they're not doing anything that would produce runoff. Just a buncha digging and clearing."

"Well, hopefully you can tell what it is then, when you see it." As Danielle spoke, the stench wafted up from the swamp again, hot and sticky decay. She wrinkled her nose, resisting the urge to cover her face with her shirt. Was it just her or had the smell gotten worse? "Aaaand here it is."

They broke through the scrubby tree line to the shore, and Danielle immediately knew something was wrong. Luca voiced it before she could.

"Was the ground like this before…?" she asked, looking over at Danielle. What had previously been rich black swamp mud had turned to dust. Clouds kicked up underfoot.

The birds had changed, too. They looked worse somehow, like poorly preserved mummies, feathers falling off as the skin underneath cracked and flaked away.

"I dunno about the ground, but you weren't kidding about the birds," said Sydney, finishing with an impressed-sounding whistle. It echoed in the small clearing, and Danielle realized just how quiet it was here. Quiet as it was when they'd found the birds. It made her skin crawl. Sydney, however, didn't seem bothered. "Must be almost two dozen here. I shoulda brought more bags."

"Have you ever seen anything like this?" Danielle asked them.

"Nope, can't say I have," Sydney shrugged. "Doug?"

"Nope," Doug shook his head, "But we both just got transferred here this January, so I can't say we have a terribly good frame of reference for this."

"I can tell you one thing, this ain't normal anywhere else." Sydney walked closer to the line of corpses, seemingly unbothered by the smell of death. "You probably already knew that, though."

"Could you ask the last people who worked here if this happened in this area? Maybe they have some record of it," Luca offered.

At that, both WMA managers looked at each other, pausing on a hesitant inhale. They turned back to Luca and Danielle.

"They kinda went AWOL," said Sydney.

"Now Sydney, that makes it sound like they just quit without saying anything." Doug chided.

"Okay, okay," Sydney held up her hands. "They didn't *officially* go AWOL. But they did disappear."

"What?" Danielle's eyes widened.

"Mmhm," Sydney nodded. "Right off the face of the earth. Both on the same day, too. No one really knows what happened. I heard they just didn't come home from work one night."

"Whatever happened, they've been treating it as a missing persons case, and we're filling in until they're found," Doug said.

"Just between you and me," Sydney gestured between

herself and the researchers, "I'm starting to think it's more of an *if* than a *when*."

VITAL SIGNS

It usually took thirty minutes to get to the nearest hospital from Big Cypress Bayou. It had only taken Harper twenty. Calling an ambulance had been out of the question. The cost wasn't so much the problem (though it definitely would've been a problem later) as the time. No way could someone get there quicker than she could get out, and getting out had been a high priority. As she'd peeled away from the swamp, old truck engine heaving with the effort, she'd sworn she still saw that thing in the trees behind them.

Harper was still calling it a *thing*, mostly because she didn't have a better word for it. Monster, maybe, but that would make the story sound crazier than it already was. The moment she had gotten through the hospital doors, she'd told them to call the police, send them out there, bring guns and EMTs and anything else they had on hand. Those hikers might still be alive. That thing might still be there. No one had hesitated. Hesitating isn't generally something people do in an ER, and they had no reason to disbelieve her. It was only after one of the police officers came to talk to her properly that things got a little dicey.

"And you said it was…how tall?" The officer, a soft-looking man who was probably more comfortable with desk duty, glanced up from his steno pad. This wasn't an officer from Uncertain, no one she knew. He was Marion County police.

"Shit, I dunno. How tall's a moose?" Harper worried her lip, trying to remember the stats her dad had told her once. She would have asked him, she would have asked him a lot of things, but he was in emergency surgery. Best not to think about that. "Eight, nine feet maybe?"

"Alright, then." He didn't believe her. He wasn't even trying to hide it. Still, he wrote something down. Harper hoped it was the truth.

A drug test wasn't far behind that line of questioning. Then it was a psych evaluation. What day was it? Who was the president? Could she spell "world" backwards? They were making sure she had a grip on reality, though she had no idea what her spelling capabilities had to do with that. Normally, this kind of scrutiny would have ruffled her feathers. Right now, it just made her tired. The adrenaline that had carried her through the swamp was gone and it left her feeling hollowed-out, like a snake skin. Brittle and empty.

"You don't believe me, do you?" Harper finally said to the ER doctor questioning her, whose nametag read Dr. Cindy Morgan. She was an older woman with a southern belle air and makeup to match – the kind of person who said *bless your heart* to call you stupid. Her smile never reached her eyes.

"I never said that," Dr. Morgan said.

"You wouldn't still be asking me questions if you believed me." Harper rubbed her face.

"This is just protocol." Dr. Morgan scribbled something onto the clipboard she was holding. "We're making sure you're alright to release."

"Release? No, I'm staying with my dad." Then, thinking better of what she might have just agreed to, she quickly added, "Though I appreciate y'all not keeping me prisoner."

"It would only be for further evaluation. But so far, I think you're perfectly fine in that regard." Dr. Morgan finally clipped the pen back to the board and looked up at Harper with that same smile. It felt patronizing.

"So we're done?" Harper shifted in her seat. "I can go see my dad?"

"You and I are done, yes, but you can't go visit him just yet-"

"Why not?" Harper blurted out, more accusatory than she meant for it to be.

"Because," Dr. Morgan continued, clearly biting back a disapproving glare, "a few of the police officers would like to speak with you."

"What? I already told them everything I know, what else do they want?"

"To make sure they have their story straight. You're the only conscious witness, after all." With that, Dr. Morgan tucked the clipboard under her arm and stepped out of the examination room. Her words hung in the air long after she left, heavy and sharp.

It felt like hours before the officers came into the room, but it was probably only minutes. The soft desk jockey from earlier wasn't with them. Instead, it was two new men, one older and one younger. The older one had scowl lines and could have stepped straight out of the '70s if it wasn't for the cellphone strapped to his hip. The younger one looked like he was fresh out of the academy, still immaculately clean-cut. There were a few chairs in the room. Neither of them sat down.

"Harper Benoit?" the older officer asked. Once Harper nodded, he continued, "I'm Sheriff Perkins, and this is Officer Flores. We'd like to ask you a few questions about this afternoon."

"Did that one guy give you my report? Or do I have to tell it again?"

"He did, but we'd like to hear it in your own words, if you don't mind." Even though Perkins seemed to be giving her an option, Harper knew damn well that he wasn't. He was just being polite. So she did the polite thing back and told the story for the third time: how the guy with the camera wandered off, what she saw when they all followed him into the swamp, the impossible chaos of it all. Both officers gave her a look when she couldn't remember any of the tourists' names, and an even uglier one when she started describing the *thing* in detail. She decided to cut that part short.

"And how did you manage to keep from being injured?" asked Flores.

"I dunno. Lucky, I guess. I think the blonde girl distracted it." At that, a chilling realization struck her. "Is she okay?"

"No, as a matter of fact, she isn't. Everyone was dead at the scene."

Harper put her hand to her mouth as a fresh wave of guilt washed over her. Somewhere in the back of her mind, she had already known they were dead. But hearing it was different.

"And yet," Perkins continued, "you manage to make it out of all this without a scratch. I'm starting to wonder if there's something you're not telling us."

"What? What are you talking about?"

"I mean, it is impressive the way you're sticking to your story, I'll give you that, but my people didn't find any wild animal out there. Certainly nothing like you're describing."

"Wait, are you saying I had something to do with this?"

"I'm saying that's a hell of a lot more believable than what you just told us. You ever heard of something like that, Flores?"

"I've heard of Bigfoot, does that count?"

Perkins gave the younger man an unamused look. "No, it does not." Then that unflinching, judgmental gaze was turned back to Harper. "But Dr. Morgan out there says you passed your psych eval with flying colors. So that tells me either you're real good at faking it, or you're real good at lying."

"I'm not *lying*, why would I make this shit up?"

"Great question, why *would* you?" Perkins crossed his arms and gave her an unimpressed once-over. "In fact, why don't we go down to the station and continue this conversation there."

"Whoa, whoa, hold on, are you seriously trying to arrest me?" Harper straightened up, trying desperately to keep the panic off her face.

"Technically, we're taking you in for questioning," said Flores. "It's a little different."

"How could I have done any of that?"

"That's what we're aiming to find out," said Perkins.

Before Harper reacted or even processed what was going on, the door opened. It was a nurse. One she had handed her dad off to. She couldn't have been older than 20, but she had the deadpan seriousness of someone twice her age.

"Sorry to interrupt, but I think you two need to come with me." she nodded at the officers, "Mr. Benoit is awake, and he's talking about a monster."

NIGHT SONG

Nature took its course much faster than Luca had expected. Faster than anyone had expected, really. By nightfall, all the birds Sydney left had turned to bone. Pale, fragile skeletons collapsing into the strange dust under them. It was the dust that bothered Luca the most. She could give the bird decomposition the benefit of the doubt – maybe a scavenger had finally picked them clean – but not the dust. There was no explanation for that, not one that satisfied her. Not when it had appeared in the matter of an hour and hadn't changed since. She had gathered a soil sample after the WMA managers left, but it would be weeks before she could get it to someone who could analyze it.

Soil. Leaves. Blood. This research project was about to turn into a multidisciplinary mess, and while there was something exciting about that, it threw the project's initial time frame out the window. So much planning to be done. So much coordinating, and she didn't even have access to Excel to organize it all. Luca's shoulders tensed up just thinking about it. Danielle was on the same page. As they sat at their makeshift workstation in the sticky darkness, they tried to discuss the future of the project.

"Okay, soooo, let's say this *isn't* a disease issue." Danielle brushed a mosquito away, scooting closer to the citronella candle in the middle of the table. Bugs sizzled as they hit its flame. "I still think the contamination theory would be good to explore. Just because it's not from an obvious source doesn't mean it's not there."

"Either way, we're going to need to get more people involved." Luca bit into the semi-sweet protein bar. Neither one of them had felt like cooking that night. They hadn't even had time to run to the state park for showers.

"I know, but we'll need to have a solid project outline if we want the funding for those people. I mean, there's barely enough grant money for the two of us, and it's not like we can keep tacking on stuff to the arbovirus study."

"Especially if it's something else entirely." Luca rested her head in her hand. "We could try to get more information from the WMA managers, maybe some data from past surveys. Maybe the old ones recorded a population decline recently, or a newly introduced plant disease or something. Otherwise, I'm not sure we have a project at all."

Danielle reached across the table to pat Luca's arm, soft hands scrubbed clean with hand sanitizer. "We have the one we're working on. That counts for something. And as soon as we finish up here, we can start outlining whatever this next one is."

"Yeah. We can just keep an eye out for anything else out of the ordinary. I still want to know what happened to those birds, though. The blood and the decomposition-"

A low, resonating call from the trees cut her off.

Chuck-will's-WI-dow. Chuck-will's-WI-dow.

Danielle gasped as she caught Luca's eyes in the dim candlelight, and Luca felt herself smile.

The squat, mottled birds reminded Luca for all the world of discount Muppets. They were perfect. Most of the birding community seemed to agree. Sure, they weren't flashy tropical birds, or even particularly rare, but they were elusive – which is the only incentive birders ever need. Saying you spotted one was noteworthy. In some circles, getting a good picture of one earned legitimate bragging rights. It was just the kind of meaningless distraction they needed right now.

Luca snatched the camera from the table and mouthed a question to Danielle. *Ready?* Danielle grabbed the callback speaker and an iPod that had seen better days and nodded. *Ready.*

This was, admittedly, not the intended use for a callback speaker. Not specifically, anyway. They were portable speakers, the sturdiest and cheapest the lab could find, connected to an MP3 player, which in turn was connected to a database filled with hundreds of bird songs. They were lures. Usually, one placed near the mist nets, just out of sight. Most birds were territorial enough to want to chase off any competitors as soon as possible and blindly flew towards their own calls before checking to see if there was a bird to go with it. Sometimes, they didn't even care if a person was still standing there when the song started. Luca had been hit by more than one overzealous cardinal throughout the years.

Luckily, Chuck Will's Widows weren't exactly aggressive. Calling it would only draw it closer to inspect the newcomer. Close enough to snap a picture if they were lucky. As they both got up, Danielle leaned over the table and blew out the candle. The darkness sunk in.

Headlamps were adjusted. Luca double-clicked the 'on' switch and the ground in front of them was bathed in red. White light was easier to see by for weak human eyes, but it ruined everyone's night vision – nocturnal animals included. It left them open to predation. Easy targets, sitting blind in the dark. Just like she and Danielle would be without their headlamps.

As the identical call came through the speakers, the bird responded in kind. If Luca didn't know better, she would have thought it sounded confused, as if it didn't expect a visitor.

Chuck-will's-WI-dow? Why-are-YOU-here?

It came from the far edge of their camp. Luca and Danielle crept over, every silent step bringing them farther into the wilderness. Moonlight shone on the water in the distance, twinkling between the cypress trees. Up ahead, the glint of a prehistoric alligator eye. Behind, the uninterrupted rustle of a snake making its way through the underbrush. And all around, the hiss of the swamp coming alive, audible even over the faux bird call trilling from the speaker.

The two songs sang in the round until it sounded like they were right next to the Chuck Will's Widow. By the red light of her headlamp, Luca caught the gleam of downy feathers. The rotund bird was cautiously shuffling through the tall grass. She patted Danielle's arm as softly as she could and pointed. In turn, Danielle put her hand to her chest and mouthed an overly dramatic *awwww*. Luca took that as her cue; she snapped the picture. The flash was blinding. She'd forgotten to turn it off, not that it mattered now. Before her vision cleared, the swamp fell utterly silent.

A hot wind blew up from beyond the trees. It reeked of old death; the dry kind, where the skin has sunken in and all the fluids have leaked out. It was familiar in a way Luca couldn't place, and she didn't have time to try. Something started towards them through the trees, following the wind, gait uneven and heavy. Luca scrubbed her eyes. It didn't help. Blotchy, pale shapes stood out in the dark and formed into something completely illogical. No animal she'd ever seen, for sure.

Whatever was walking towards them hissed low as it came closer. Something clicked under the noise, like bone on bone. It started moving faster. Luca grabbed Danielle's arm and yanked her off to the side as the creature burst through the tree line. She didn't stop moving to look back at it. Neither did Danielle. They bobbed and weaved through the campsite, seals to a shark, heels skidding in the dirt, thundering footsteps following them. There's no way they could outrun it much longer. Humans were made to be endurance predators, sure, but that only worked out when you were the ones doing the hunting; the theory didn't account for you being prey. Not unless you used tools.

Luca veered sharply to the opposite edge of camp where they'd parked the truck, pulling Danielle along. Danielle didn't ask why. She didn't have to. Luca nearly ran into the side of the truck before she pulled the door open and shot inside, dragging Danielle with her.

Danielle scrambled to push down all the locks, reaching across the driver's side as Luca patted around for the keys.

"C'mon, c'mon. Where are they…" Luca strained to reach under the bench seat. It would be so much easier if she could open the door and look from outside.

"Do you have the keys?"

"If I had the keys, we'd be out of here already," Luca snapped.

"Then where'd we put them??" Danielle leaned over into the backseat to look, her small stature making it difficult to reach the floor without tipping onto her head. Luca considered asking to switch jobs.

"I don't *know*. Where did we last have them?"

"Well, last time I saw them, they were in your backpack."

Luca froze. Her backpack was under the canopy. Outside.

"Shit." Luca's stomach dropped as she looked out the window. The strange, bony thing that had chased them was still out there, pacing around the truck. Watching. Waiting. Even with clear vision, it didn't look real.

Danielle sunk back into her seat. "Ooooohhh my god, we're trapped." Her voice shook with adrenaline. She looked over to Luca. "Do you know how to hot-wire?"

"What? No, I don't know how to *hot-wire*."

"Hey, it was worth a shot!" Danielle glanced out the window, then shrunk further into her seat. "I don't think we have a lot of options here."

Luca ran her hands up her face and through her cropped hair. Deep breaths.

"Okay. So. We can't move the truck, and we can't leave the truck." Luca turned off her headlamp and slipped it back around her neck. Even the red light felt too bright now. "We don't know what kind of animal that thing is, or whether it can eat us."

"Deer can't eat people, but they can still kill them." Danielle said, switching off her own headlamp. "Maybe now that we're out of sight, it'll get tired of waiting and leave."

"Maybe. If we survive this, we're keeping the keys in the truck from now on." Outside, the creature hissed again, that low radiator whine. Luca shivered despite the heat. "Tonight, I think we'll have to sleep in the truck. I'll take the first shift."

RANGER STATION

Daylight was a welcome change. The intense sun burned off the sick fear that had lingered over their campsite all night, ramping up the temperature in the already-stuffy truck cab. Danielle was drenched in sweat that she wasn't hydrated enough to be losing, but suffocating heat was better than staring out into the darkness, waiting for death. Or having the darkness stare back.

Danielle had barely slept last night, even when it was her turn to. Every time she'd gotten comfortable, a noise outside had jerked her awake. A shuffle. A hiss. The softest scrape of bone against metal. After a while, she hadn't even been sure if they were real or her imagination. Peeking out the window had rarely confirmed which was which. Even when she couldn't see the thing that had chased them, her mind filled in where it might be hiding in the dark. In the tree line, behind their tents, in the blind spot of the truck. It could be out there waiting for them to get too relaxed, like a mountain cat stalking its prey.

Her shift had been the last one, and she'd waited until the sun was far enough above the trees to call it over. Just in case. When it was finally bright enough outside, she leaned into the backseat where Luca was curled up.

"Luca. Hey, wake up. It's morning." Danielle reached out and tapped her. A soft sigh came as a reply.

"Yeah, I know," Luca rolled over to lay on her back and groaned.

"How long have you been up?"

"Too long." Luca scrubbed her face. "Is it all clear out there?"

"Mmm, I don't know." Danielle shifted back to the front seat to look out the windows. "Maybe? I can only see so much."

Begrudgingly, Luca sat up to look out the back windows. "I don't see anything out this way. Want to open the doors?

"Not really, no."

"We'll have to eventually." Luca started to crawl up front, an unwieldy process considering that the truck had bench seats. "We can't live in this hot-ass truck."

"I mean, we could live in it a little longer." Danielle tucked her feet up onto the seat as Luca settled in next to her.

"Listen." Luca put a hand on Danielle's shoulder, firm and confident. "If it's still out there, we just shut the doors again, okay? We'll be faster than it, especially since it's not close enough to see."

"We don't even know what *it* is. How do we know how fast it is?"

"It's some sort of wild animal. We beat it once, didn't we? And that was outside." A soft pat, and Luca leaned over to peer outside through the front windshield. "Hell, I bet if I was quiet enough, I could snag the truck keys from under the canopy and we could actually get out of here."

"What? Oh my god, *no*, are you crazy?" Danielle huffed. "Let's just…let's just peek out the door and check first, okay?"

"That's the spirit." Satisfied, Luca grabbed the driver's side door handle. "On three."

Danielle nodded, grabbing the other door handle with sweaty hands. "On three."

One.

Two.

Three.

They opened the doors together — fresh air rushing into the truck, Danielle bracing for the worst. Only an empty campsite and eerie silence greeted them. The thing was gone. The heady stench of decay was gone. That awful ragged hiss, gone. In fact, there was hardly a sign that it had been there at all.

For the briefest of moments, Danielle hoped that it had all been a dream, or a hallucination, or Dickensian food poisoning, but the ground around the truck told a different story. What had been dry, packed dirt was now dust, littered with tracks she had never seen before. Hooves with too many points had dragged around their truck innumerable times. When she got out to look closer, she saw that it had left a dent in the side of the truck, like it had been hit with a sledgehammer. Danielle's heart skipped a beat.

"Luca...c'mere." She heard her voice shaking.

"What is it?" There was an urgency in Luca's voice as she stepped around to Danielle's side of the truck. The tension fell away from her like a heavy coat when she saw that there was nothing to run from here. Danielle almost felt bad for scaring her like that, but all of this was just as important as seeing the creature itself. This proved what it could do. "Well, shit. This is going to be fun to explain to the rest of the lab."

"Yeah. I'm not sure our car insurance covers this kind of hit-and-run," Danielle worried her lip. "What are we gonna tell them, anyway?"

"I don't know." Luca shook her head.

They stood there for a long moment just looking at the truck. Taking in what had happened. In the daylight, the remnants were surreal. Danielle felt like if she touched it, it would disappear. So, she did – and it didn't. The metal was rough and grainy where the creature had scraped off the paint, like it had already started to rust.

Danielle took a breath and broke the silence again.

"Do you really think it was a wild animal?"

Luca paused for so long before answering, Danielle almost repeated herself.

"Let's just get back to work."

And that was it. After they figured out that nothing but the truck was damaged, and whatever that thing had been was long gone, they did try to get back to work. Nets were opened, blood was drawn. The longer the day wore on, the more last night felt like a nightmare rather than reality. But it was a nightmare that lingered. Every time Danielle heard a noise in the underbrush or caught a flash of movement in her periphery, she jumped. Luca was doing the same thing, though she pointedly refused to talk about the incident again. They had other things to worry about, she'd said, and it didn't matter now. Danielle wasn't so sure.

When midday approached and all the birds settled into their hiding spots to wait out the heat, Luca and Danielle decided to do the same. Except instead of the cool shade of cypress and pine, they retreated to the state park's showers.

Field work until the heat of the day. Showers at the local park. More field work until dark. It kept them feeling mostly clean without sacrificing productivity. Danielle wasn't keen on the working-until-dark part tonight. It might be safer to retire early, or even to sleep in the truck again. They hadn't discussed that yet, though. They didn't discuss much of anything on the way there. The whole ride was spent in silence – Danielle had tried to put on music, but nothing felt right, so she turned it off. Fleetwood Mac wouldn't get them through this one.

Halfway through the drive, she ended up occupying herself by flipping through the camera's pictures. They had taken plenty on all their prior, but they'd never reviewed them. Most were of the birds they'd caught interspersed with pictures of the field sites, each other, and crew members who had joined them temporarily. And the picture from last night. She lingered on the earlier ones when she remembered that, dreading what she might see. When she finally worked up the courage to flip to the final photo, it didn't live up to the hype she'd built up in her mind. The picture from last night was just a bird sitting in the grass, overexposed by the flash. It would have excited her yesterday. The picture was clear, arguably not bad, but it proved nothing. There was no strange creature, no teeth, no bones. Danielle wasn't about to announce what they'd seen to the world — telling a story like that would be career suicide — but she would have liked more proof, just for herself.

Arriving at the ranger station was a relief, if only because now Danielle had something else to do.

"I'll be right back." Danielle hopped out of the truck to go renew their parking pass.

"Got it. I'll wait for you here." Luca busied herself with grabbing their shower bags from the back seat as Danielle walked away. The showers were a long trek from the ranger station.

Danielle pressed her hand against the glass door of the station, and her fingers grazed paper. She paused.

There were two pieces of paper taped haphazardly to the glass, wrinkled printer paper and bright yellow cardstock. The printer paper was a missing poster. It showed a pair of boys, no more than thirteen or so, skinny and scrubbed clean for school pictures.

Mason Evans and Sawyer Evans

Last seen May 22nd

Have you seen these boys?

Of course she hadn't. But they'd only been missing a few days. That was a positive note – one she decided to focus on instead of how hopeless a search out here in the sprawling wilderness must be. She'd keep an eye out.

She would be keeping an eye out for a lot of things, if the yellow cardstock was to be taken seriously, too. It was a warning about a bull running loose in the swamp.

REPORT TO LOCAL AUTHORITIES. DO NOT ENGAGE.

Sounded a bit dramatic for a domesticated bull, though she supposed that was better than encouraging people to catch it themselves. The desperate, logical part of her brain wanted to turn what she'd seen last night into a bull. Twist the memory until it fit a paradigm she preferred. But she knew that would be a lie.

The cool, stale air of the ranger station rushed out to meet Danielle as she finally pushed open the door. A little bell chimed. Low fluorescent light cast the knickknack-lined shelves in strange shadows, and

Danielle realized just how long it had been since she'd set foot in a building that wasn't a park bathroom or a run-down gas station. She felt a little like Tom Hanks in Cast Away, minus the volleyball. Luca was a lot better than a volleyball, even though Danielle could probably have talked through her anxieties more with Wilson.

But right now, they were going to pretend things were normal. It was easy here. Everything looked like it should, pristine and faux rustic. Even the park ranger behind the counter fit the aesthetic, crisp and clean-cut from head to toe, like an adult boy scout. He was an efficient one, too, renewing her parking pass in less than a minute. It took longer for her to get the card reader to work.

"So, you enjoying your vacation?" he asked, rehearsed and chipper.

"Yeah, we are – but it's not actually a vacation, it's field work. I'm a biologist." That was easier than saying ornithologist to most people, since saying *ornithologist* opened up a whole line of questioning that revolved solely around the definition of the word. Sometimes she even just resorted to *scientist* when the situation called for it, like when she had to buy dry ice from a local Kroger and wanted to avoid weird looks. *Scientist* got you a pass on a lot of things.

"Really? What're you studying out there?"

"Birds, mostly. My colleague and I are doing a disease study."

"Good, tell me if you guys find out what's going on out here. Seems like there's way less birds around than last year."

"Sure thing, you'll be the first to know." Danielle opened her mouth to ask him if he was a birder, but the question died when she heard raised voices from the back of the station. Ever so casually, she glanced over her shoulder. The park ranger behind the counter was not so casual about it.

From what looked like an office, another ranger was escorting a young woman out. Danielle couldn't make out details from where she stood, but she could hear every word.

"I'm sorry about what happened, ma'am," The ranger's voice was purposefully even, "But I already told you, we can't just shut down a state park –"

"You mean you *can't* or you *won't?*" the young woman, who was most definitely Texan, spat.

"I mean *both*. I don't have the authority to do that, and it's almost Memorial Day weekend. We're not just going to kick all of these people out."

"So you're gonna let them die?"

"No one's going to die—"

"Yes they *will*, you ain't listening! There's something big and dangerous out there, and it's gonna hurt people if you don't keep 'em away!"

Now she really had Danielle's attention. Sure, she might just be a local nutjob (a concern reinforced by the ranger's warning that, if she kept talking, he was going to consider this a threat), but it felt irresponsible to ignore her after what happened last night.

Danielle watched from the corner of her eye as the stocky park ranger urged the much taller woman out of the station. As he started to close the door on her, she stopped it with her foot.

"Just 'cause you don't believe me doesn't mean it's not there."

She moved her foot and the door swung shut. The entire station fell silent.

WORK ZONE

Duke usually liked his job. He didn't like that this one was in northeast Texas.

The sun beat down mercilessly the moment it rose. By 10 a.m., Duke was sweating. By noon, he wanted to find somewhere dark to curl up and die. He wouldn't be the first thing on the jobsite site to do that. It'd been less than a week and they'd found two dead possums in different pieces of equipment, curled up impossibly in the guts of the machines. They'd drawn straws to determine which unlucky bastard had to scrape the dead thing out.

It was one of the many snags in what should have been a straightforward job: shifting around dirt and trees until there was enough room for massive steel pipes to lay. Everything moved was deliberately set aside; the dirt was piled close to cover up the future oil pipeline, and the trees were cut and stacked to sell later.

The pieces too small to sell were put into a burn pile just to the right of the trench. Not that they could burn it in a drought like this; Duke wasn't sure what they were going to do with it now. It wasn't even good for sitting on in the meantime. (One guy had tried it and fallen right on his ass.) Their only option for sitting during breaks was the real timber or the ground. Duke wasn't too jazzed about either, considering the snakes and bugs he'd seen around here. But both were better than being slow-roasted in the cab of the Bobcat, so he went with the timber. Hopefully it was too newly stacked to have attracted critters yet.

One of his coworkers, Earl, had the same idea. Earl wasn't exactly his favorite person. He smoked while he ate, which seemed like a waste of a good cigarette and food, and he spit too much. But Duke couldn't afford to be picky about his company these days. He was running out of coworkers to choose from.

"You seen Curtis today?" Duke unscrewed the lid of his thermos. Lukewarm coffee and a pimento cheese sandwich, same as every day.

"Nope," Earl flicked his almost-empty lighter a few more times before he finally lit his cigarette. He took a long drag. "Haven't seen him since yesterday, actually."

"Figures." Duke shook his head. "That asshole probably left for Memorial Day thinking we got vacation or something."

"Or he just quit without saying nothing. Seems like the type." Earl waved his cigarette in one hand, digging into his lunch bag with the other.

"Seems like a lotta people are quitting without saying nothing right now." Duke fidgeted with polyester strap of his own lunch bag.

"What d'you mean?"

"Well, like. You remember that one guy? Oh... Leonard what's-his-name. That one who came in early and worked late like a goddamn maniac."

"Yeah, I figured he was looking for an excuse to not go home and couldn't find a bar anywhere around here." Earl popped the top off his soda can.

"But then one day he just didn't show up, and he hasn't showed up since. What makes a guy like that quit all of a sudden?"

"I dunno. If I had to guess, I'd say it's because this site's the biggest train wreck I've ever worked at. Machines breaking left and right, dead shit turning up everywhere, and now we're running on a skeleton crew." Earl ashed his cigarette terrifyingly close to the log they were sitting on. "Hell, if I could afford it, I'd quit, too."

"Yeah," Duke took a bite of his sandwich to buy himself time and look around for their supervisor, just in case he took the talk of quitting too seriously. "I gotta say, me too. I can't wait for us to move up on out of here. Never worked in a place with so much bad luck."

Earl made a noise of agreement as he took a bite of his own food. Between that, cigarettes, and diet soda, his mouth should have been too busy to talk for a while. But Earl found a way to get words in edgewise.

"Hey, you see that?" Earl leaned over to Duke, cigarette smoke still wafting out of his mouth. His gaze was fixed on the far side of the trench where trees still stood.

Duke shaded his eyes from the noonday sun and peered out across the strip of newly cleared land. Something was walking in the woods, but what he was seeing couldn't be right. It looked like it was made of bleached bones.

"Yeah," said Duke, "What is that?"

O U T   T H E R E

"Hey, um. Excuse me? Do you have a second?" Danielle held up her hand, half in greeting and half in apology for interrupting whatever this chick was doing. In the middle of the gesture, she caught sight of the state of her own fingernails and quickly lowered her hand. Oh god, they were so dirty. Even during the field season, when it was difficult to avoid, she couldn't stand for her fingernails to be dirty. But when the woman turned around, it became clear that she probably didn't care about the state of Danielle's nails.

The young woman was tall, taller than Danielle by a head or so, with a burnt-on farmer's tan and permanently muddy work boots. She looked like she'd been living in the woods as much as Danielle did, maybe more so. Like she belonged in a post-apocalyptic movie. Danielle could picture her standing there with a shotgun, hair perfectly tousled for a promo shoot, a smudge of fake dirt on her cheek. A rugged kind of pretty. In real life, the woman stood there with decidedly imperfect hair and something on her cheek that was either real dirt or odd freckles.

For a moment, Danielle was fixed with that same glare the woman gave the park ranger, but it softened almost immediately as they met eyes. "What's up? You need directions or something?" She still looked a bit stand-offish, but Danielle was starting to think that was just her face.

"Oh, nooo, no. I just." Danielle fiddled with the hem of her shirt. "Couldn't help but overhear you talking to the park ranger about something in the swamp?"

"Alright, I know how that sounded, trust me." The woman held up her hands. "But it's true. There's something out there."

"Yeah, I believe you. That's why I wanted to talk to you."

"Wait. Seriously?"

"Seriously." Danielle glanced around for eavesdroppers, then leaned in closer. "I think I saw it, too. Or. I saw something. It was definitely weird. And big."

The woman's eyes lit up, somewhere between terror and excitement. "How big? What'd it look like?"

"It was, uhh…" Danielle reached her hand as far above her head as she possibly could. "Taller than here. Like a big buck or-"

"A moose?" The woman asked.

"Yeah! Like a moose! I mean, I've never actually seen one in real life, but that sounds right. It was a lot spindlier though." Danielle wiggled her fingers, as if that would help get across the message. It apparently did.

"Holy shit. How the hell'd you get out of there in one piece?"

"We ran." Danielle shrugged, as if thinking about last night didn't fill her with paralyzing dread. "And my field partner and I might have spent last night in the truck."

"Field partner?" The woman looked at her like it was a euphemism for something. Danielle had to bite her lip to keep from laughing.

"Yeah. I'm a biologist. We're doing research out here. Or, we're trying to. I'm Danielle, by the way."

"Harper. Good to meet someone who listens." Harper held out her hand. "Sorry you had to, y'know, almost die, though."

Danielle wiped her hand on her pants one last time and hoped to god she was right about Harper not caring about the dirt when they shook hands. Hers were rough and warm. Confident. Danielle's heart skipped a beat.

"Hey, at least we didn't actually die. That counts for something." Danielle shrugged, feigning an ease that she never really had. "How'd you get away?"

"Running." Harper glanced at the ground. "Same as you. Probably just lucky, too."

Danielle took a long breath. "What do you think it was?"

"I dunno. Could be anything. All I know is that it's killing people, and it needs to go."

"How do you know that it's killing people?" The moment the question came out of her mouth, Danielle wanted to pull it back.

"I've seen it."

Danielle's stomach dropped. That was the last answer she wanted, and it was the one she knew she would get.

"I'm so sorry-"

"Thanks." Harper's answer was clipped, and Danielle almost apologized again for asking. Instead, she floundered for another subject.

"Do you, um. Do you wanna keep in contact about this? Like, if one of us figures something out, or if you need help, or…"

"Yeah." Harper's face softened once again, if only a little. "That might be a good idea." There was the hint of a smile. Danielle smiled back.

They exchanged phones, Danielle's pastel pink case contrasting sharply with Harper's scuffed gray one. Danielle typed much faster. While she waited for Harper to finish chicken-pecking her number in, she looked up and caught eyes with Luca, who was giving a quizzical look from the truck. She felt her cheeks flush and looked away. When they traded phones back and their fingers brushed, she saw Harper's whole face do the same.

"So. See you around?" Danielle asked.

"I sure hope so."

After a few moments of the awkward goodbye shuffle, Danielle scurried off to the field truck. Luca met her with a conspiratorial grin.

"What was that all about?" Luca papped her arm. "Did you just get a girl's number?"

"Oh my god, shut up, no." Danielle covered her face. "Well. Yes. But it was about the thing we saw last night. Mostly."

Luca's mood immediately shifted, dropping back into the same gravity she'd had this morning.

"Really? How so?"

"She saw it, too." Danielle was still blushing, but she matched Luca's tone. "And she says she saw it kill people."

"Oh, shit. That changes things." Luca breathed. "We should call Sydney and Doug to tell them that something's going on. They need to at least know that they should be alert out on the WMA."

"Definitely. And maybe be specific about what that something is." Danielle knew that Luca was on the same page as her about keeping their reputations intact. Luca gave her a look that said as much. "Just a little specific. It's important."

"Alright, I'll just tell them to be on the lookout for a wild animal. And I'll call them from the truck." Luca climbed back in and shut the door behind her. After a minute, Danielle was about to get into the driver's seat and turn on the truck for her for the sake of A/C, but Luca was stepping out before she could. "I had to leave a message. But they're the only two at that office, so it shouldn't be a problem."

"Yeah. Hopefully they're not out there right now."

"Hopefully not." Luca tossed Danielle her shower bag and grabbed her own again. "Hopefully they call us back before we're back in a dead zone."

ON RECORD

One missed call. 4:23 p.m.

Luca's phone screen flashed as they passed over the bridge that led to the WMA. She hadn't heard her phone ring. Neither had Danielle, clearly. It only registered that a call had come in at all when it picked up on a stray scrap of signal floating around rural Marion County.

"Could you check that?" Luca asked, barely glancing away from the road.

"Sure thing." Danielle typed in the passcode without having to ask. They spent too much time together for her not to know it. "Oh. Looks like it was the WMA office." A few more taps, and a message began to play over speakerphone.

"Hey, Luca, it's Sydney. You probably already knew that, but…anywho. I got your message. We gotta talk. Y'all meet us at the office." A little breath. The shuffle of Sydney's sunburnt cheek on the receiver. "You ain't gonna like what we found."

Silence filled the truck cab as the message ended. Dread crept down Luca's spine like a centipede, steady and disquieting. She pulled into the next dirt drive and turned the truck around in three swift movements without saying a word. She didn't need to. As much as she hated spur-of-the-moment things, they had no choice right now.

Unlike everywhere else they'd been, the office was in town – though calling it a town was generous. The main stretch of Uncertain wasn't much more than a few houses, a post office, a diner, and train tracks that ran into the horizon. Nameless streets and sun-bleached stop signs. The bone-dry shoreline of a tributary that should've connected to Caddo Lake. Luca hadn't even seen any people. If not for the parked cars, she would've thought there weren't any at all. The WMA office, tucked away on the far edge of town, looked as deserted as the rest – but that wasn't surprising. Luca had never seen a busy wildlife management *anything*.

"I hope everything's okay." Danielle shook out her hair as she hopped down. Droplets of water flew off. In this humidity, it was going to take hours to dry. "That message was kinda… ominous."

"Yeah. I'm not holding out hope."

It was dim as they stepped into the lobby, even though the lights were on. Office lights could never compare to sunlight. There was something weirdly comforting about the place, though, empty and dark as it was. It reminded Luca of a library. Musty air mingled with old books and coffee, the cheap '90s carpet muffling their steps. Dioramas and posters lined the walls, all nature-themed, as if a visitor might drop by at any moment. As they walked towards the offices proper, they passed the biggest one: "Animal Tracking: Try It on Your Next Hike!" Luca paused there, only long enough to glance at the tracks pressed into fake mud behind the glass. None of them looked like the tracks they'd seen this morning.

When they approached Sydney's office, there were finally signs of life. Quiet bubbling from a coffeemaker and hushed, intense chatter. Slightly brighter lights. (Or maybe Luca's eyes were just adjusting.) Before they could announce themselves, Sydney greeted them, energetic as ever.

"Hey! There y'all are. We were starting to wonder if you'd gotten the message. Coffee and cookies are up for grabs if you want 'em." She gestured to a small table off to the side. Instead of single-use cups, there was a precarious tower of mismatched mugs next to the coffeemaker.

"Oh, hell yeah." Danielle made a beeline for it, only slowing down when she carefully plucked a mug from the stack.

"Thanks. I'm never gonna say no to coffee. Or food." Luca followed right after Danielle, who was already busy shoving a little cookie in her mouth.

"Oh my *god*, these are good." Danielle didn't bother to finish chewing before talking. No one here had any illusions of decorum.

"Thanks, I made 'em myself." Doug smiled, eyes crinkling proudly.

"You're gonna have to give me the recipe. I need these in my life."

"Watch out. You get him sending you one recipe, he's gonna send you a dozen," said Sydney.

"I'm so, so okay with that," Danielle waved her hand.

"Me, too, as long as I get stuff without having to do any of the baking," said Luca.

"You might, if I don't eat it all first." Danielle snatched another.

Once they had all settled down with their coffee and food, Luca broached the real reason they were there. She'd rather keep up the meaningless chatter all day. She'd rather this not be happening at all – but her rathers didn't matter here.

"So, what did you find?"

"Well…lotsa stuff." Sydney shuffled through papers and books on her desk. "First thing's first, I gotta say that your call wasn't the first one we got about this. I mean, WMAs down here get a lotta calls this time of year. Usually, it's hunters asking where they can and can't go – but this year it was about a lot more than that."

"We got calls from all sorta folk," said Doug, "Hikers, bird watchers, pipeline workers."

"And they weren't just calling about where they could go," said Sydney. "They were all reporting some kinda big animal roaming around, one that looked outta place. A lot of 'em called it, like, a deformed white bull."

"One person thought it was a 'weird llama'." Doug added.

"Y'know," Danielle clicked her nails against her coffee cup. "I saw a sign that said to be on the lookout for a bull that had gotten loose at the ranger station."

"Wait, really?" Luca turned to her. "Why didn't you tell me?"

"I got sidetracked!"

Luca gave her a knowing look, and Danielle was suddenly very preoccupied with her coffee.

"I can't blame anyone for thinking it's that, or blowing it off," Sydney continued, "Most people thought it was an escaped farm animal. Or an albino they thought they'd get some kinda credit for spotting," She waved her hand. "Anyway, we looked into it.

Called all the farmers in the surrounding areas, made sure they had all their livestock accounted for."

"Did they?" Luca asked.

"Well..." Sydney made a vague hand gesture and looked to Doug.

"They didn't have any missing, so to speak. But they'd been having a lot more than usual turn up dead. So, they were technically all accounted for."

"Technically." said Sydney. "But that gave us something else to look into. We talked to most of 'em about going and testing their livestock for disease since they're so close to the WMA, but some of the livestock was turning up all dried and weird, not just regular dead."

"So that made us think of what y'all showed us a few days ago," said Doug, "Y'know, the birds."

"Which got us to wondering how abnormal either of those incidents are around here. It's not like either of us have seen very many seasons in this particular spot," said Sydney, "So we started looking at records. And we found a hell of a lot more than we expected." She snagged a seemingly random folder, slim and new, and plopped it on the desk in front of them. "You remember those WMA managers that were here before us? The missing ones? They left these."

Luca hesitantly reached forward to open the folder. It was filled with incident reports, progress reports, and unformatted typed papers, all dated. At a quick glance, they all had to do with one thing: a large, unidentified animal in the swamp.

"Did they figure out what it was?" Luca asked.

Sydney shook her head.

"How, um. How close are these dates to when they went missing?" said Danielle.

"From what I could gather, pretty damn close. Too close for them to leave us a lotta details. So we had to look a little harder." Sydney rummaged through the papers again and pulled out a battered yellowed notebook. "And then we found this."

She opened it up, like a teacher with a picture book, and flipped through a few of the pages while she talked. Most of it was beautiful, unreadable scrawl, peppered with sketches – plants, animals, and lots of map sections.

"This thing's been buried in the bottom of our storage closet for god knows how long. It's from the

'20s, probably a cartographer or something. Maybe a naturalist. Heck, maybe it was for the railroad company building here. We dunno, the writer's unclear about that, and front page where the name should be is missing. Anywho. They wrote about what was going on at the time, what they found out here. It was-"

"Eerily familiar." said Doug.

"Exactly," said Sydney, "Drought, construction problems, animals and plants dying in ways they shouldn't – people dying."

"Just like-" Danielle started, looking over at Luca.

"Just like that girl said." Luca was breathless now. All of this felt like a dream. Irrational, bizarre, yet somehow still maintaining a vice-like grip on her heart.

"It's terrible, really." Doug shook his head. "And it just ain't normal."

"We were actually talking about it earlier this morning." Sydney took the notebook back and thumbed through it. "And then you called us, Luca, and told us what y'all saw. And suddenly something made a heck of a lotta sense."

Sydney turned the notebook back towards them, and Luca's stomach dropped. Danielle's hand flew to her mouth. There it was, in pen and ink – the creature they'd seen last night. It was unmistakable. Tall and bony, ill-proportioned. Like someone shook up an alligator and a buck and stripped off the flesh.

"Holy shit…that's." Luca ran a hand through her hair. "Okay. Why aren't there more accounts of this? An animal that big in a populated area should have been officially discovered by now, especially if it's been around since the 1920s. Probably longer, realistically speaking."

"We thought the same thing." said Doug, "But the person writing this said it disappeared as soon as the drought ended, and I guess no one's seen it since."

"But that doesn't make sense," Luca said. "Species die out when the climate changes, yes, but they don't suddenly come back. They stay dead."

"This one apparently doesn't," said Sydney. "If it's a species at all. We couldn't get accounts of more than one being sighted at a time."

"Hold up. Are you insinuating that it's the same animal? From the '20s? That's ridiculous." Luca did her best to sound firm, but everything was coming out tinged with nervousness.

"Luca," Danielle said, "Have you ever seen an animal with that much exposed bone, walking around? Have you ever seen anything like what we saw last night?"

"No, but that doesn't mean it's as old as the Dust Bowl!" said Luca, "Besides. It was dark, and there was a lot going on – who knows what we saw."

"You and I both know what we saw." Now it was Danielle's turn to give her a look, unusually firm. "Just because it doesn't make sense to us right now, just because it doesn't fit the paradigm that we're working in, doesn't mean we can write it off."

The air in the office was heavy as they met eyes, Danielle daring her to disagree.

"Alright," Luca started, tentative. "There is something out there, we know that. So, let's say everything you guys said about it is true. How do we deal with it? We can't exactly make it rain."

"Gotta admit, we didn't get that far." said Sydney. "We just know you two need to get up out of there. Getting funding for the WMA ain't worth your lives."

"But what about the other people out here?" Danielle turned back to Sydney and Doug. "The tourists? The hunters? The pipeline workers? Aren't they in danger, too?"

"And this thing sounds like a really destructive invasive species." Luca said. Putting it into a category she understood made it feel more reasonable, more real. Like something they could handle. "It might be putting everything here in danger. We can't just let it run around unchecked."

Doug nodded sagely, stroking his mustache. "Guess we're gonna have to do something about it, then."

SHOTGUN
SHELLS

Seeing her dad was much nicer without all the police around. In fact, Harper would be fine if neither of them ever had to talk to the police again. Once they'd decided that she wasn't a murderer, the police shared the sentiment. The Caddo Lake park rangers probably did, too, now. Harper was good at burning bridges with authority – with everyone except her dad. She spent every second of visiting hours with him, even though he wasn't awake for most of it. His odds were looking good. Better than they should, really, considering the severity of his injuries. The doctors had told her that he just needed to rest, and she believed them enough to not try to wake him. All she did was hold his hand and hope they were right.

But she couldn't do that forever. Sitting there. *Waiting.* What was she waiting for, anyway? For more people to die? For that thing to wander into town? For it to go away on its own? Harper had a hard time believing the last one. Problems never went away on their own. They either played themselves out or got worse until they were impossible to ignore. She didn't like either option in this case.

The cops weren't going to handle it, that much she knew. Neither were the park rangers. Danielle – whose soft sincerity and dark eyes still made her heart flutter – and her field partner seemed like they had science stuff to worry about. That left her. What was she doing?

Nothing. Not yet.

"I'm gonna fix this." She gave her dad's hand one last squeeze as she got up. "I promise."

Harper had planned on staying until visiting hours were over – maybe even overnight, if they didn't kick her out – but she wasn't waiting any longer. Right now, she had about an hour left of light. An hour was all she needed. Twenty minutes from the hospital to the swamp, speeding down the back roads, shotgun rattling in the rack behind her head; twenty minutes to plan as her truck struggled to keep up with her demands, engine wheezing as she pressed harder on the gas. Forty to execute it. She could have done with even less. The plan was simple. Shoot it.

She pulled off the main road to weave down wooded trails towards the newly dried-out hiking paths, branches smacking against the truck like they were trying to hold her back. Maybe they were. Eventually, the road became too narrow, even by her standards. The truck skidded and shuddered as she shifted to park without stopping first. Dust still swirled around her tires as she hopped out. That thing had been here. She was sure of it.

It was darker under the cypress canopy, what little light there was left struggling to push through the leaves and Spanish moss. Harper made sure her gun was loaded as she waited for her eyes to adjust. Five shells in the chamber. Five more in her pocket. That should be plenty to take care of business.

As she walked down the trail, shotgun at the ready, the swamp was disconcertingly quiet. Unseasonable dead leaves crunched underfoot. The only noise was a distant bird song, calling the others home for the night. Harper joined it with a long, beckoning whistle.

"Hey, you out there?" Her voice felt too loud, but last time the thing came around there was a bunch of people. A lot of noise. "I'm alone." She raised her voice. "Defenseless!"

She braced herself for those thundering footsteps, that whining howl. But the swamp remained empty, silent save for her own voice calling out into the deep, wild nothing. Dark was approaching fast. She needed to do something different.

"Fine. Maybe this'll get your attention." She cocked the gun and fired off a deafening shot into the sky, scattering leaves and bits of branches from the canopy overhead. It left her ears buzzing, cicada-harsh, in the following silence. That was all there was. Silence.

"Come on! I know you're out there!" Harper cocked the gun again. "Come and get some!"

Silence again.

"Oh, now you're shy, you little chickenshit? I said come and *get some!*" She fired again. Nothing. For a second, she was starting to believe the police reports. Maybe it was just some wild animal, one that was scared of gunshots like everything else. Maybe she was being irrational.

Then the wind blew up. That hot decay from the hiking trip mingled with newly airborne dirt, and Harper's doubts faded. It was real. It was pushing towards her through the scrubby underbrush. Her heart skipped a beat as she cocked the gun again. As it emerged from the tree line, Harper set her sights square at center mass and fired.

The creature didn't react. It was like she didn't even clip it, even though she'd seen the leaves in front of it obliterated. It just lumbered closer. She saw details now: skeletal arched back and a long maw, bones barely covered by strips of flesh. The walking corpse of an impossible animal.

She took another shot. Her ears were still ringing, her shoulder still reverberating, but the way that thing was reacting, she might as well not have been shooting at all. She convinced herself that maybe she was just missing. It had been a while since she did target practice, and the air, full of dirt and acrid rot, stung her eyes. Missing this thing was entirely possible. Even twice in a row.

But now she saw the whole thing clearly. It was only 30 feet or so away. This time, she aimed for the head, praying for a clean kill. Buckshot ricocheted off its long, bony skull.

Harper's stomach dropped. She tried to shoot again, quick, center mass.

Click.

The chamber was empty, and the creature was closing in. She cursed as she shoved her hand into her pocket, fumbling for bullets. It would be better to pop one into the chamber and put the rest in the magazine, a process she could do with her eyes closed, but she could only do it standing still. She only managed to get one round in the chamber before the creature got too close for comfort and she had no choice but to run. Only when she'd gained a little distance did she dare to turn around and shoot. The creature barely flinched. So she kept running.

It was an exhausting, inefficient pattern. Run a few feet. Turn around. Put one in the chamber. Pump. Fire.

Run, turn, load, pump, fire. None of the shots slowed it down, even though she saw them hit. Every time she stopped to fire, it gained on her a little more.

The last bullet hit it square in the chest. Scattered buckshot dented its strange, exposed bone. The creature paused. For one brief, desperate moment, Harper hoped. It let out a hiss, a dying radiator. Then it charged again. Harper almost dropped her shotgun as she turned on her heels, running full-speed in the opposite direction.

She tried to work her way back to her truck, but the creature kept pushing her farther and farther from it. Farther into the swamp. So far in that she didn't know where she was, and she sure as hell didn't have time to suss it out. Was it smarter than she'd thought? She was barely staying in the lead. She almost missed the dip of a small creek as she wove around a tree, regaining her footing at the last second. Somehow, it had managed to stay filled with water. Now she definitely didn't know where she was.

With the running start she couldn't help but have, she cleared the creek, not wanting to risk being slowed down by wading through. Slowing down could cost her life. A few seconds after she'd crossed it, another unearthly roar echoed from behind her – it sounded pained. Without stopping, she glanced back. It was the creature, one leg in the creek, steam curling up from the water.

Before she could process that, before she could even look in front of her again, her boot caught on something and ripped the earth out from under her. Her face hit the ground with a teeth-rattling *thunk*, and her shotgun clattered against a nearby tree, but the rest of her landed on something that muffled her fall. Something that crunched sickeningly under her. The smell of rot was overwhelming. Harper scrambled to her feet, her stomach churning.

On the ground in front of her were the bodies of two boys, no older than thirteen, in hunting gear. Two boys she knew from town, their skin brittle, hollow sockets where their eyes should be.

DRY ROT

At twilight, the swamp exhaled. Luca wished she could exhale, too, but her breath was permanently caught in her throat. It would be until they got all the nets down, she told herself. Until the entire camp was disassembled and Caddo Lake was in the field truck's rear view. Then she could relax. Maybe. Holding onto that idea helped take the edge off the anxious buzz – but she knew the idea was flawed, so it didn't work for long. There should be a step between taking down camp and leaving. Luca just didn't know what it was going to be. The uncertainty might kill her before that creature did.

That was a thought she was still getting used to. That there was something out there she didn't even come close to understanding, something too dangerous and strange to study – yet. Even though it looked like they'd have to kill it for the sake of the ecosystem and everyone else, Luca couldn't bear the thought of *never* coming back. If this thing was out there – completely unstudied and unknown – there were inevitably more things to discover lurking in the dark.

Considering what they knew so far, though, the current priority was to get out. Make a base camp elsewhere and figure out how to deal with this strange invasive organism from there. Sydney and Doug were right – the last thing they needed to be doing was catching birds. Not only was it dangerous for them, but it felt cruel to trap anything in the same place as that creature, even if it was only temporary. Plenty of things were dying out here without their help.

Taking down nets together was a routine, muscle memory at this point. She got on one end, Danielle got on the other. They took the tall metal poles apart into their manageable pieces, slipped the net off, rolled it up, and put it in a bag. The only hard part was prying the rebar that held the whole thing up out of the ground. It took wiggling it back-and-forth with a mallet until the dirt decided to let the iron rod go. Luca was almost tempted to leave it, but it would've been a hazard to the wildlife. Even under a time constraint, that wasn't an option she was willing to consider.

Their routine had gone uneventfully for the whole camp, nets and all. Luca assumed that it would be the same for the last net, too. There was daylight left, if only in slivers that shone through the bows of the cypress, and things felt deceptively normal. Until she touched the net. The normally tightly woven rope frayed as she ran her hand over it. Danielle dropped her end, and as Luca looked up, she saw it was because it had just... Fallen apart. Dry rotted. Even in the heat, she felt a chill run down her spine.

"Nope. Nope, nope. We're getting out of here *right now*." Danielle picked up the bottom half of the pole, the rest of the net falling away. Now that Luca was looking a little closer, she saw the metal had the lightest coating of rust.

"Jesus, I didn't think it could do that to something inanimate." Luca crumpled the remains of the net into a ball to tuck into the bag, suddenly aware of how little they could see around them. "Do you think it's still here?"

Before Danielle could reply, footsteps pounded to their left, first quiet then quickly getting louder, and something burst through the scrubby tree line. Danielle swung the pole she held at it and there was a thud as whatever it was ducked and hit the ground.

It was too small to be the creature from last night. In fact, it wasn't a creature at all. It was a woman – a tall, lanky woman who had barely avoided Danielle's swing, and now was scrambling to get up.

"Holy shit – Harper?!" Danielle dropped the pole and went to help the struggling woman up. "Ohmygod I'm so sorry, I didn't know it was you."

"*Danielle?*" The woman, apparently Harper, stared up at Danielle.

"Wait. Is this that girl you were telling me about?" Luca asked, and Danielle nodded. Then she turned to Harper. "What the hell are you doing running around out here?"

"No time. We gotta go." Harper shook her head. With Danielle's help, she got to her feet. She looked like she was about to fall out, taking great heaving breaths between every clipped sentence.

"Why?" Luca knew the answer before Harper had to say it. As she turned her gaze to where Harper had come from, she saw movement in the distance. The crash of hoofbeats. Luca dropped the net and closed the distance between herself and the other two. "Never mind, we're going."

She grabbed Danielle's arm, trusting her to drag along Harper. The trust was well-founded. They ran for the campsite with Luca leading the chain. Branches smacked her face as she passed and the thorns of half-dead greenbrier tugged at her pants. She felt someone lagging, probably Harper, but that just made her pull harder. Run faster. She was prepared to carry someone if she had to. Hot wind beat at their backs, bringing with it that familiar whiff of death. Hoofbeats edged closer and closer every second.

The pale silhouette of the field truck came into view. With one last burst of energy, Luca broke through the underbrush and into the clearing, barely stopping in time to open the driver's side door. She started to shove Danielle and Harper into the truck, but they didn't need help. Danielle was already dragging Harper in as soon as Luca let go of her arm. Luca slid in after them, shutting the door behind her. The slam of the door was followed by another loud bang. The truck rocked. Danielle yelped, and Harper clung to her. Luca had to hold on to the steering wheel to avoid sliding into the driver's-side door.

She snatched the keys from the dashboard. The engine roared to life and she hit the gas, heading for the main road. Dust kicked up behind them. As they sped away, the creature let out an unearthly howl like a drill grinding against bone.

DARK WATERS

The truck was a three-seater only in theory. In practice, Danielle found herself scrunched in between Luca and Harper, knees hitting the part of the dashboard that clearly wasn't constructed with someone sitting here in mind. It made it even harder to catch her breath. As if all the overwhelming aspects of the situation were made physical in the claustrophobic cab. She looked over to Luca to see if the feeling was mutual; she was glaring at the darkening road ahead, jaw set. Then she looked over to Harper. Their eyes met in the dim light, and in hers there was fear. Sick fear and relief and something else that Danielle couldn't place. A hopeful, detached part of her wanted to call it affection. Maybe in another life.

"What the hell were you doing out there?" Luca snapped. It made Danielle jump, but then she realized she was talking to Harper. "Danielle said you knew how dangerous this thing was!" The more agitated Luca got, the harder she pressed on the gas, engine revving as they sped towards the highway.

"That's why I was out there!" Harper snapped back, gesturing widely. Danielle dodged her arms. "I was tryna kill it!"

"How did it not kill *you?*" Luca asked.

"Hell if I know! It probably should have! Only reason I got ahead of it was 'cause it tripped in a creek and… I dunno, hurt itself? And I… I." Harper's voice wavered. "*Fuck.*" She dropped her head into her hands, arms tucked back in like a dying beetle.

Danielle felt the tension on her skin, the air prickling like it did before a storm. Waiting for the first crack of lightning to set it all off. When she reached over to touch Harper's shoulder, she half-expected to be shocked. Instead, Harper looked up like she just remembered she was in a car with other people, eyes wet.

"I found the Evans boys while I was running," Harper started up again, choking back the tears that threatened to fall down her dirty cheeks. "Y'know those missing kids? The ones that disappeared a few days ago?"

Danielle nodded. She remembered the poster from the station clear as day, and the memory draped over her in a thick, uncomfortable blanket of dread.

"They're dead." Harper put her head back in her hands, running them down her cheeks this time. Danielle could have sworn she was shaking. "They're fucking dead and I'm gonna have to tell someone. God, what if I have to tell their *parents*?"

"Oh my god. I'm so sorry." What else could she say to that? She wanted to reach out and touch Harper's shoulder again, but she felt she'd met the comforting touch quota already. Any more might just make things worse. Hugs always made her cry. "But I don't think it's your job to tell their parents. I mean, we'll tell someone, but not them. Probably the police."

"We will. But first, we're getting rid of that thing." said Luca, posture still sharp, but the edge to her voice had softened.

"How are we gonna do that? *Bullets* didn't do anything." said Harper. "I shot it and it just fuckin' stood there!"

"You said it hurt itself in a creek, right?" said Luca, "I think we can make it do that again."

"I think we're going to have to do more than hurt it." Said Danielle.

"We're going to do a lot more than hurt it. We're going to drown it."

"Okay," Danielle said in a way that definitely wasn't agreeing to whatever Luca had planned, "first we need to figure out where we're going right now."

"We can stop at my place." Harper offered, voice still crackling with emotion. "It's pretty close. Closer than the ranger station."

"Alright," Luca nodded. "Direct me."

Directions were the only things said on the way there. Harper was clearly trying to reel in her composure, and the less she talked, the further she got from crying. By the time they got to her house, she almost seemed like she'd pulled herself together.

Harper's house looked tired. Like it had been a house too long, its wooden slats sagging with age. There was an attempt at a garden, choked with new weeds, and an old truck Danielle didn't recognize with a cheesy "My Other Car is a Boat" bumper sticker on the back. Said boat was hitched to it.

Harper awkwardly led them in, making a vague 'well, here it is' gesture before hurrying to swipe a pile of mail off the little kitchen table. Danielle wondered what it all was, but decided that that wasn't her business. She muttered something about the house being nice instead, and Harper thanked her. Luca didn't bother with compliments. As soon as they were offered a seat, she started hashing out a plan.

First, she decided that they should compare notes. Harper quickly ran through what she hadn't already told them, how powerful and deadly it was, how it had purposefully chased her away from her truck. In turn, Luca and Danielle gave Harper the rundown of what they'd found out at the WMA office. The drawings in the journal, the strange industrial correlations — how old this thing might be. It felt unreal. Like someone was going to come in and tell them that this wasn't real, monsters weren't real. It was just a bull, or a big cat, or a bunch of awful coincidences. Under the eerie campfire glow of the kitchen light, Danielle could almost convince herself it was a ghost story. Almost. But Luca kept talking, and the monster stayed real.

"We can drive it into the water," she said. "The field truck could withstand getting hit by it before, it can probably take it again."

"But how are we going to get it to come to us in the first place?" said Harper.

"Noise. I'm not sure exactly what all attracts it, but we know noise does. We still have the callback speakers with us. That might do the trick."

"What if the truck doesn't work?" said Danielle. "None of us have tried chasing it before."

Luca paused, tapping her fingers on the table, then looked to Harper. "Can you pilot that boat out front?"

"Sure, I do it all the time — or I did."

"You could wait with it near the water's edge, then lure it out into the lake when it gets close. Do you think you could do that?"

"If that's what it takes to kill it, yeah. Yeah, I can."

It was decided. Harper would pilot the boat, Luca would drive the field truck, and Danielle would operate the speakers from the other truck. Foolish and foolproof all at once. Danielle didn't bring that up as she rode with Harper back to the swamp, callback speakers piled on her lap. She didn't bring anything up at all. Every topic she thought of felt out of place, either too casual or uncomfortably serious. They just shared a few nervous glances, an accidental hand touch that made Harper's cheeks turn red. A silence that weighed so heavy that Danielle thought she might collapse under it.

Driving to the water through the strange, winding paths cut for fishers was nerve-wracking, and she found herself gripping her seat. The path was suffocatingly narrow. Every branch that hit the trucks sounded like a gunshot. Every step seemed to echo as she and Harper pushed the boat into the water. Her own heartbeat pounded in her ears as she hung the speakers with sweating hands. The swamp was too quiet. That was never a good sign.

Danielle crept back to the truck, barely shutting the door behind her with a light *click*. She pulled her knees up to her chest and scrolled through the bird calls on the busted-up iPod. Tried to slow her breathing. This, at least, was something she had done before. Pick the right call, attract the right animal. So, she picked the loudest bird on file, a red-shouldered hawk, and turned the speakers all the way up.

She watched the narrow road anxiously from the truck parked by the water. The cars were off, and barely a sliver of moonlight came through the cypress. The swamp was still. Dark. Silent. There was only the hawk call, that cacophonous screeching coming from every angle, and the speakers swaying in the breeze. It didn't do a lot for her anxiety.

They could have waited seconds, or minutes, or half an hour. It was impossible to tell, just watching the darkness between the trees. Danielle's muscles were so tense they could snap.

Then the creature burst through the trees with a bone-shaking crash. Danielle clapped her hand over her mouth as she watched it try to headbutt the speakers. The cords connecting them to the trees withered at its touch and dropped to the ground. Crackling static replaced the hawk call. One by one, it took out the speakers until only one was left. One just on the edge of the water. Hope swelled in her chest as it edged towards the shore, knocking the last speaker to the ground. Harper started up the boat engine. The creature looked over at the noise — then it turned away and started to walk back into the trees.

The field truck roared to life, headlights blinding as they shone on the beast. Instead of backing up and being forced to the water, though, it charged.

Luca revved the engine and met it halfway. The truck and the creature took up the entire dirt road, and they met with a terrible crunch of metal and bones. Mostly metal. When the creature reared back, it was clear it had put a significant dent in the truck. Still, Luca pushed on, trying to press it back. Danielle tried to turn the speakers on again, but nothing worked, and the thing didn't care about the guttural rumble of the boat engine. Danielle couldn't tell, but Harper might even be shouting. Her silhouette was waving her arms frantically, trying to get the things attention. No dice. It only cared about the truck, and it charged again. This time, Danielle heard glass crack. Fear squeezed her chest – Luca could get hurt. She could die.

Danielle's legs moved before she had time to second-guess herself. She dropped the iPod and bolted out of the truck.

"Hey!" She skidded to a stop on the trail behind the creature.

Luca yelled something from inside the truck, muffled. It sounded like "what are you doing," but Danielle couldn't tell, so she ignored her.

"Hey! Over here!" Every word was a struggle to get out of her throat.

The thing turned on its heels, impossible joints clicking as it looked at her with its hollow skull. That same fear squeezed her chest again, making it impossible to breathe, but she ran anyway. Ran from the pounding hoofbeats, from the withering heat beating down on her back.

Her foot slipped when it hit the water, the slick mud unexpected after yards of dry dirt. By the time she scrambled to her feet, the thing could almost reach out and touch her. It got harder to run the deeper she trod. Her height did little to help. Soon she couldn't touch the bottom anymore without her nose dipping under, muddy water threatening to come in with the air.

Splashes obscured what little she could see in the dark. She swore she felt the thing step down not inches from her, its massive frame making waves that threw off her balance, when her arm was grabbed and yanked. Harper pulled her up onto the boat. Danielle hit her knees, gulping air, as Harper hurried back to the steering wheel. They sped further out onto the lake and away from the creature. It took a few more gangly strides before jittering to a halt. In the glow of the field truck's headlights, Danielle saw its silhouette standing still. The beginnings of steam clouds rose up from the water around it.

"Stop, stop, look!" Danielle frantically patted Harper's arm until she stopped the boat and turned around. The rumble of the boat engine faded. In the near-silence, she heard it — the creature hissing like hot metal plunged into cold water. It was sinking. Dissolving, piece by agonizing piece. Danielle didn't blink until its skull sunk into the lake.

"Do you think it's…?" Harper's voice was barely above a whisper, as if talking might make the thing rise back up out of the water.

"I don't know," Danielle shook her head, voice just as soft. "Let's go check on Luca."

Harper swung the boat in a wide circle around where the creature had sunk. Danielle swore she could still see the water bubbling in the moonlight. She tore her eyes away from the space as they reached the shore, scrambling over the side to get to Luca, who was still hanging half out of the truck.

"Are you okay?"

"Yeah." Luca hopped down from the running board, voice quivering with adrenaline. "I think so. Are you?"

Danielle nodded.

Satisfied, Luca looked over to Harper, who was bringing up the rear. "You?"

Harper nodded as well. Luca let out an audible breath. Before anyone else could speak, Danielle pulled them both into the tightest hug. She felt tears roll down her already-wet cheeks. Felt both of the other women shaking. For a long moment, the only noise was the pounding of their hearts — then, finally, the swamp started to hum once more.

AFTERMATH

Uncertain sat motionless in the thick early June heat. Too late for lunch, too early for dinner, the diner was empty aside from a bored waitress and two customers: Danielle and Harper. The coffee break was supposed to include Luca, too, but she'd managed to get out of it at the last second. Said she needed to talk paperwork with the WMA managers before she and Danielle headed home, that they shouldn't wait up for her. There was coffee at the WMA office, and no, they didn't need to come with her. They should just enjoy themselves at the diner.

It was a set-up if Danielle had ever seen one. A set-up that made her very nervous, but after almost dying, the anxiety was mild in comparison. They'd found themselves alone in a cramped little window booth, ordering coffee and attempting to make small talk. Danielle had stared at the table for the entire first half of the conversation. There was a gash in the laminate where someone had picked at the edge, revealing the cheap wood underneath. An unidentifiable sticky spot near the condiments. An attempt at carved initials that had been given-up on halfway through; the ghostly outline of a couple's initials, heart and all, that someone couldn't be bothered to finish. When Danielle finally looked up, she caught Harper eyeing the same spot.

Her dad was on the mend, Harper had said, which put her in better spirits. He was even talking about doing tours again. That Harper wasn't so sure of, but she'd give it a go if he was willing to. The real question was whether any customers would be willing to go out there, after everything that had happened.

Funerals were being planned for the Evans boys, delayed by investigations that had no satisfying conclusions. Memorials were held for the college kids, remains still waiting to be sent back home. Danielle wasn't going to any of them. It felt intrusive, especially since Harper — her only real connection to any of the dead — didn't ask her to come. People deserved to grieve without strangers watching. There would be more than enough strangers asking them questions soon. News crews were going to descend any minute. More people had been declared missing within the last week, all pipeline workers, all last seen before Memorial Day. The disappearances, combined with the mass walkout they'd triggered, had indefinitely halted pipeline construction. As much as Danielle wanted to be glad for the construction stopping, she couldn't be. The victory felt hollow. Not a victory at all.

"Do you think they…y'know. Do you think they'll ever find those guys? The construction workers?" Danielle fiddled with a flimsy paper napkin, glancing back down at the gash in the table.

"Dunno. The swamp has a way of swallowing up things like that, even when it's dry."

They both fell silent as the waitress came by to refill their coffees, as if she couldn't hear every word they said when she was leaning against the front counter. She did a good impression of not hearing, though, responding to their thanks with a little nod before getting right back on her phone.

"So," Harper continued as the waitress walked away, "do you think you'll ever come back here?"

"Maybe. The project is pretty much finished, but there's always next field season." Danielle tapped her cup with freshly scrubbed fingernails. "Or, you could come up to Oklahoma and visit us. When you're not busy with work or anything."

"Yeah," A small smile played on Harper's lips. "I think I'd like that."

As Danielle reached for the sugar, her fingers brushed Harper's. Neither one of them pulled away. Through the window, sunlight glinted off the waves lapping onto the nearby shore, a newly filled tributary running strong. Danielle looked up, and she saw it was the same color as Harper's eyes.

Thanks for reading! Please leave a short review on Amazon and let me know what you thought!

Honest reviews are incredibly powerful. They help others find my work, they help me make a living, and they tell me what you'd like to see more of. (Or less of!)

ABOUT THE AUTHOR

B. Narr is an Oklahoma-based writer who may or may not just be a bird who learned to type. When not writing, you can find B trying out new bread recipes, running obstacle course races, and roaming the nearest state park looking for cryptids.

www.bnarr.com

ACKNOWLEDGMENTS

There are a lot of people to thank here. Like, a lot. Hopefully, I managed to get everyone in.

First off, I need to name the names hinted at in the dedication. I've worked with a lot of biologists, and pieces of them keep popping into my work, but without two in particular this book wouldn't have even happened. Thank you Tamaki, for being a wonderful mentor, a friend, and the coolest ornithologist I know. Thank you Krisangel, for the amazing weeks in the field, for the long car ride sing-alongs, and your indispensable knowledge. I couldn't have done it without you two.

Thank you to everyone at the Caddo Lake State

Park and Caddo Lake WMA for having the most gorgeous swamp to do ornithological research in.

Of course, I need to thank my family here for their incredible support. I couldn't have done it without them, either. My mom, for bearing with me through every painstaking revision, and for helping this story make any kind of sense. My dad, for your intense perfectionism and eye for detail on the final product. Ryllie, for keeping me grounded and never sugar-coating your opinions. Trever, for answering all my hunting and oil field questions, no matter how obnoxious. Thank you all, I can't say how much I appreciate you.

My amazingly creative friends, thanks for blindly championing me. I don't know what I did to deserve your undying support, but I'm not gonna look that gift horse in the mouth.

Thank you to my beta readers, for giving me feedback and the confidence to put this book out into the world. Apo, for being ridiculously supportive and a fellow horror nerd. Susan, for your kindness and attentiveness. Cindy, for your incredibly detailed notes and scientific perspective. Kathleen, for giving horror a chance and your editorial insight. Linda, for helping me evoke more emotion and clarity. Mary, for your honesty and structural notes.

And thank you to the team that helped put this book together. My editor Ryan, who made this book ready for the public eye. Thank you for your swamp folk knowledge, your horror knowledge, and fixing my terrible dialogue formatting. My cover artist, Eric, who gave it the gorgeous cover to be judged by. Thank you for working with me and listening to all of my requests, however vague they were. You're both awesome.

Last, but certainly not least, thank you to everyone reading this. You're what makes all of this possible.

CPSIA information can be obtained
at www.ICGtesting.com
Printed in the USA
LVHW050831261119
638501LV00007B/493/P

9 781734 021806